GHOSTLY LOVER

Crime and Passion
Novella

Mary Lancaster

DRAGONBLADE PUBLISHING, INC.

ARE YOU SIGNED UP FOR DRAGONBLADE'S BLOG?

You'll get the latest news and information on exclusive giveaways, exclusive excerpts, coming releases, sales, free books, cover reveals and more.

Check out our complete list of authors, too!

No spam, no junk. That's a promise!

Sign Up Here

www.dragonbladepublishing.com

Dearest Reader;

Thank you for your support of a small press. At Dragonblade Publishing, we strive to bring you the highest quality Historical Romance from some of the best authors in the business. Without your support, there is no 'us', so we sincerely hope you adore these stories and find some new favorite authors along the way.

Happy Reading!

CEO, Dragonblade Publishing

Additional Dragonblade books by Author Mary Lancaster

The Duel Series
Entangled (Book 1)
Captured (Book 2)
Deserted (Book 3)
Beloved (Book 4)

Last Flame of Alba Series
Rebellion's Fire (Book 1)
A Constant Blaze (Book 2)
Burning Embers (Book 3)

Gentlemen of Pleasure Series
The Devil and the Viscount (Book 1)
Temptation and the Artist (Book 2)
Sin and the Soldier (Book 3)
Debauchery and the Earl (Book 4)
Blue Skies (Novella)

Pleasure Garden Series
Unmasking the Hero (Book 1)
Unmasking Deception (Book 2)
Unmasking Sin (Book 3)
Unmasking the Duke (Book 4)
Unmasking the Thief (Book 5)

Crime & Passion Series
Mysterious Lover (Book 1)
Letters to a Lover (Book 2)
Dangerous Lover (Book 3)

The Sinister Heart
The Vulgar Heart
The Broken Heart
The Weary Heart
The Secret Heart
Christmas Heart

The Lyon's Den Series
Fed to the Lyon

De Wolfe Pack: The Series
The Wicked Wolfe
Vienna Wolfe

Also from Mary Lancaster
Madeleine
The Others of Ochil

CHAPTER ONE

T ENDRILS OF CLOUD drifted across the moon, bathing a swath of the countryside in a pale, almost shimmering silver. The tired carriage horses, as though smelling their oats, picked up speed again. To the right, through the trees, Griz glimpsed a large, gracious house, and the knot in her stomach tightened with a rush of nerves and anticipation. Now she and Dragan would be together again. She had missed him, and his summons to join him at Cathlinn House had been balm to her unexpectedly lonely soul.

Of course, she should have gone with him in the first place, but the journey with a fractious baby from London to her father's seat in the Scottish borders had exhausted her. Truth be told, she had been a trifle miffed when Dragan had left her only a couple of days after arriving at Kelburn, when he had received a letter from a friend in Renfrewshire. She had refused to go with him.

But then a slightly desperate note from him, including an invitation from his hostess, had brought her charging across the country, complete with teething infant, who at least had the grace to be contentedly asleep as they approached their destination.

The coach charged up a steeper hill, swinging around narrow bends, with high walls on either side, which was when Griz noticed the castle for the first time. Perched on the hill to her left, surprisingly close to the road, the picturesque ruin of a square keep rose into the sky. Perhaps disturbed by the carriage, two bats flew across the moon, and beneath it, against the outline of the stone walls, she saw a couple embracing.

It was a romantic, atmospheric place for a tryst, though Griz would not have cared for the presence of the bats. This couple did not seem to notice them. As the carriage breasted the hill, the woman wound around her swain seemed a willowy wisp of loose blonde hair and pale, flowing garments that looked weirdly insubstantial in the moonlight. Griz had missed such embraces herself, so she generously wished the lady joy.

Until her male companion turned his head toward the carriage, and she saw that he looked very like her husband.

And then the coach swerved around the bend and downhill with another burst of speed. The road rose on up the next hill, but the horses turned right into a winding drive toward the big house she had noticed earlier. And if the couple at the castle ruin didn't quite flee her memory, she could at least laugh at her mind for playing tricks on her.

Cathlinn House was a pleasant country home of two stories and attics beneath the eaves, small, perhaps, by the standards of a duke's daughter—which Griz was—but more than grand enough for a physician's wife, which she also was.

As the coach pulled up before the front steps, she pushed her spectacles more firmly on to her nose and prepared to greet her hosts. And her husband.

Ewan, her own coachman—or at least her father's—had opened the carriage door, let down the steps, and helped her and the baby down before anyone emerged from the house. Then servants spilled out to welcome her and take her bags inside.

She followed a footman inside the house. The entrance hall blazed with light, as did the central staircase, down which glided a smiling woman.

"Mrs. Tizsa, welcome," she said, crossing the hall with one arm languidly extended. "I am Claire Cathlinn. Was your journey awful?"

"No, surprisingly pleasant. Thank you for inviting me." She took her hostess's hand with a slight curtsey.

"I doubt you'll thank me when you hear what we have involved your husband in, but we are glad to have you with us, at all events. And this must be young Master Tizsa. Dragan has missed him."

I hope he missed me, too, she thought crossly, the little tableau at the castle ruin entering her head and being dismissed. She was not jealous by nature, and she had no reason to be irritated by her hostess, who was married to Lord Cathlinn's son and heir.

"Good," Griz said. "Then he will be glad to deal with the next teething crisis."

Mrs. Cathlinn laughed. "That's the spirit. You will be hungry after your journey, so a supper tray will be sent to your rooms. Oh, I have just put you with Dragan, so I hope that is acceptable to you? It was his suggestion, but we can move you in the morning if you prefer more privacy."

"With Dragan is fine," Griz said. "Thank you. I'm sorry for disturbing the household so late."

"It isn't late at all," Mrs. Cathlinn said dryly, "but the family retires early to our own rooms so that we don't need to see each other more than necessary. There is no nursery set up, but Dragan said a cot in your own rooms would serve."

"Of course. I hope he does not disturb you."

"Oh, the guest rooms are well away from mine, and besides, in this house, a little more shouting will go unnoticed."

By this time, they had reached the upper floor and turned right along the passage. Griz was rather intrigued by Mrs. Cathlinn, who was, perhaps a few years older than her, and rather beautiful in a dark, sultry kind of way. More to the point, she seemed unusually open and deprecating about her own household, though in a humorous kind of way.

No wonder Dragan had asked for help.

Her hostess led her to the last door in the passage and threw it open without knocking. At least she did not go inside.

"Your rooms, Mrs. Tisza. Supper will be up directly, and you must ring if you need anything else." Her gaze flickered over the sleeping baby. "A maid, perhaps, to change him?" she hazarded.

"No, I will manage, thank you."

"Then I shall bid you good night and look forward to seeing you tomorrow. You will meet the rest of the family at breakfast, but at least you will have Dragan to support you through the ordeal. Sleep well."

"Good night," Griz called after her retreating form, torn between amusement and vague irritation. For some reason she did not like the other woman using Dragan's Christian name, though she refused to dwell on the reason.

Closing the door firmly, she turned to examine a small, comfortable sitting room, lit by a solitary lamp and the wood fire that burned behind a guard in the grate.

"Dragan?" She walked around her bags, which had been left in the middle of the floor, toward the open door of what was, presumably, the bedchamber. Was he asleep already that he had not come to meet her?

She had to light the lamp in the bedchamber, which showed her an empty, still-made bed, and a scattering of Dragan's things—a coat over the back of a chair, books on the bedside table—but no sign of Dragan himself.

The baby wriggled, and a familiar stench assailed her nostrils. He opened his eyes and smiled as though he had been particularly clever.

"I suppose you want more food, now?" she said. "To make up for the loss."

He kicked his little legs, so she laid him on rug on the floor while she dug out the baby paraphernalia that took up most of her baggage and changed his napkin.

When the maid brought her a generous cold supper with wine and a pot of tea, she asked the girl, "Is Mr. Tizsa downstairs? Does he know I am here?"

"There's nobody downstairs, ma'am," the girl said with a strong, local accent. "If he's with Mr. Richard, I'll send him along to you."

"Thank you."

Richard Cathlinn was the younger son of Lord Cathlinn, an acquaintance Dragan had made while in Edinburgh and Glasgow for medical lectures. It was at Richard's mysterious behest that he had come here to Cathlinn House, and Griz was eager to know why—quite beside wanting to see her husband. So far, it was hardly the delighted reunion she had envisaged.

Young Alexander did a lot of kicking and throwing himself on to his stomach, then stretching up his neck to admire the scene from a different angle. Fortunately, he seemed in much better humor, though his previous tantrums must have exhausted him, for his eyes soon began to close again. Griz changed him for bed and laid his sleepy form in the cot provided. He didn't seem to notice its strangeness, for he was asleep in no time.

She unpacked the bags.

And still Dragan did not come.

She went to the bedroom window and looked out over the formal garden to the trees, between which she could glimpse the road winding uphill and the castle ruin at the top. The castle ruin where she had seen someone who had looked like Dragan.

It was not him, of course, but she was damned if she would sit here and wait for him to notice she had arrived. With sudden decision, she strode to the bell pull and rang. By the time the same maid appeared, she had donned her traveling cloak once more.

"I shall only be half an hour at the most, but please sit with the baby until either I return or my husband does. If he wakes, just stroke his forehead until he sleeps again. Will I need a key to get back into the house?"

"Oh, no, ma'am. The front door is never locked until midnight."

Griz nodded, thanked her, and left.

⋙⋘

DRAGAN TIZSA SMELLED orange blossom, and immediately, the uneasy dreams swimming through his mind vanished. Without opening his eyes, he smiled.

"Grizelda."

"Dragan. I knew you would remember eventually."

Her familiar, welcome voice was amused, and yet just a little clipped, as it tended to be when she was annoyed and did not wish to be. It was also so dear to him that he reached for her before he had even opened his eyes. And closed his arms around cold, too-fresh air.

Damn but it's freezing in here. He opened his eyes to dark sky and clouds drifting like fingers across a pale moon. Abruptly, he sat up, totally disoriented, a dull pain throbbing behind his forehead. "What the…?"

Through the darkness, his gaze at last found his wife, crouched a foot away from him. She wore a traveling cloak, the hood drawn up over her hair, her spectacles faintly gleaming.

"You came."

"Some time ago. You chose an odd couch."

"I did, didn't I? I don't even remember falling asleep. What time is it?"

"About half-past ten, I think."

He scrubbed his hand over his face and hair. This was not quite as he had envisaged his reunion with his wife. For one thing, there was still a good twelve inches between them, and she showed no inclination to close it. For another, he should never have brought her here, and the knowledge chilled him from the inside.

He shivered, rubbing his arms. He was not even wearing an overcoat. He moved his legs, trying to get feeling back into them before he stood. "Shall we go back?"

She rose, and he forced himself to his feet. He staggered on his chilled limbs, and her hands immediately shot out to steady him. His arm fell across her shoulders, and he embraced his warm, sharp, achingly sweet wife. A frown tugged at her brow and vanished. She would save her questions until he was warm, and for that he was grateful. Although she would not be pleased when he sent her away again.

But still, she smelled of Griz, orange blossom, and other delight. He bent his head and kissed her mouth because he could not wait for that. A quick, relieved kiss that was never going to be enough. He kissed her again, and this time her lips parted in welcome.

"Dragan, you are freezing, you idiot," she whispered.

"I know. Come."

Without releasing her—he needed her there in the circle of his arm, against his numb body—he walked with her down the hill from the castle and across the road toward the house. The movement helped, but he was shaking as if he had an ague. He must have slept there in the cold for almost two hours. Unforgivable stupidity, besides leaving Griz to arrive alone among strangers who were eccentric at best.

But then, so was Griz. And eccentric hosts could not discompose this duke's daughter.

He retained enough sense to lead her back inside through the side door by which he had left and use the back staircase that emerged just opposite his rooms. Their rooms.

He opened the door, and Jeanie the maid jumped up immediately from the armchair by the fire. "There you are. Your wife...oh. She found you." Jeanie effaced herself, though Griz, ever practical, called after her. "Some more tea, if you please."

"You brought Alexander," he said in wonder and dread, gazing down at the sleeping baby, who smiled as though even in slumber he recognized his father's voice. Fresh panic surged and he squashed it for later.

"Of course, I brought him. He's not a piece of luggage I can simply leave with my parents."

Prickly.

A blanket landed over his shoulders, and she pushed him back toward the fire. She removed the guard to let out more of the heat and threw her cloak over the sofa while he sank into the warm armchair so recently abandoned by Jeanie.

"Is that what you think?" he asked curiously, "that I abandoned you and Alexander like luggage?"

"Didn't you?" She knelt on the rug before the fire, holding her hands out to the rosy glow. A small flame reflected in her spectacles.

Off-balance and curiously disoriented, he could only answer honestly. "I don't know. Not like luggage. I answered a call for help from a friend, or at least a friendly acquaintance. You didn't appear to need me."

She shrugged. "We existed without each other for decades. Of course, I don't *need* you."

He let that go for now. She was far too tense and so was he.

She said, "What the devil were you doing up there?"

He frowned, and since he didn't know, he made his best guess. "I went to look for inspiration. It's where the girl died."

She stared. "What girl?"

Just for a moment, he barely knew. The vision of a pale, silvery beauty from his dreams slid along his mind and vanished. "Richard's betrothed. She died at the ruins, and no one knows how or why. That is why he sent for me."

"And why you went. Why did you send for *me*?"

"Oh, lots of reasons," he said vaguely, gazing into the fire. He made an effort. "The puzzle is beyond me. These people are beyond me. I hoped you would understand them better. And then…that's mostly excuse. I missed you."

She met his gaze, and with some shame, he read the hurt and hope there. "Did you?"

He smiled ruefully. "I went too quickly, didn't I? Another two or three days and you would have come with me. April Weir would be no less dead."

She did not touch him, which he regretted, though she admitted, "My family, en masse, is a lot to put up with. Somehow, I never thought that bothered you."

"It didn't," he said in surprise. "But when I got Richard's letter, I thought you would appreciate the excuse to enjoy time alone with them."

"I don't—" she began, then broke off as a knock on the door heralded tea.

Dragan, his bones beginning to feel warmth again at last, rose to take the tray from the maid, who curtseyed and left. Griz put a little table beside his chair, and when he had set down the tray, she poured him a cup of tea.

He sat, resuming the blanket, and received the fine porcelain cup and saucer from her in silence. He sniffed the tea, tasted it, and relaxed just a little.

"You don't what?" he prompted, when she had knelt on the floor once more.

She waved that aside with her teaspoon. "Who was the lady at the castle?"

"Lady? When?"

"I saw you with her from the coach when I arrived."

He frowned. "No, I went alone." Or did he? Something tugged at his memory and gave up. He shivered. "It's a weird place at night, though. The castle."

"I see. It's certainly a trifle weird to find you asleep out of doors in the dark."

"I did feel very tired," he recalled vaguely. Trudging up the hill with an intent he could no longer remember, the castle grim and yet misty. Dream or reality? "I was...a little lightheaded, so I sat down for a moment against a stone wall. The next thing I knew, I could smell orange blossom and knew you had come at last." He paused, shaking his head, and took a mouthful of hot tea. "Very strange dreams, though."

"Perhaps a courting couple disturbed you."

"Perhaps. The locals seem to think it's romantic, though I imagine a woman dying there might have put a stop to such trysts."

"What happened?" she asked.

"Her name was April Weir. She was engaged to marry Richard and had been staying here for a week or so before her parents were due to join the party. Her father is a merchant of some kind, wealthy, but not aristocratic like the Cathlinns."

"Did the Cathlinns approve of the match?"

"So far as I can tell. Old Lord Cathlinn seemed indifferent. Richard's brother Robert said he liked her. Claire—Mrs. Cathlinn, Robert's wife—did not. However, it was Claire who noticed April was not in her bed and raised the alarm. They found her over at the castle, almost where you found me. Only she was curled up in a ball, her arms over her stomach, and quite dead."

Griz shivered. "Had she been attacked?"

"No, not that anyone could see. Apparently, she had a weak heart since birth. The doctors believed the condition better, as sometimes happens in adulthood, but her death is being treated as natural causes."

"Then why did Richard Cathlinn send for you?"

"Because he thinks there is more to it." Dragan hesitated. "He thinks something supernatural happened to her. That some malevolent spirit took her."

Griz held his gaze. "*You* do not think that."

"There are many kinds of malevolent spirits," he said flatly. "In the living, from my experience, more than the dead."

"You believe she was murdered," Griz said slowly.

"Because of her heart condition, and because both families wished it—Lord Cathlinn is not nobody—no autopsy was done immediately. I...used my influence and insisted. In fact, I was there."

"And?"

He held her gaze. "She was poisoned with arsenic. Which is why you and Alexander must leave in the morning."

CHAPTER TWO

"WHAT?" GRIZ STARED at him. "We have only just arrived. You asked for my help."

"I did. I only discovered today that April had been poisoned. I wrote to you at once not to come, on the off chance that you had not already left Kelburn." He set down his cup and leaned forward to take her hand. "Griz, that girl was poisoned *in this house*. You cannot be here."

"But you can?" she said indignantly.

"Someone has to discover who poisoned her, for I'm pretty sure the Cathlinns control all the authorities hereabouts."

"But murder, Dragan! They surely want the culprit found?"

"Not if it's one of them."

"But surely they cannot cover this up! If arsenic was discovered—"

"It is not unknown for ladies to take small quantities to improve their complexions. That is their explanation for the presence of arsenic. Her maid concurs."

"But you don't believe it?"

He shook his head. "Something is *wrong* in this house, Griz. I thought you could help me see what, but I should never have brought you here."

She pulled her hand free. She should not be hurt. Warning bells of suspicion should not be sounding in her head. This was not how things were between her and Dragan. She said, "You and I have faced many dangers together. We look after each other, but you do not coddle me. It is one reason I chose to marry you."

"And Alexander?" he said tightly.

She stared at him. "Who would poison a baby? Come to that, who would be stupid enough to poison two people in the same house? That really would cause scandal." She stood. "I am tired after my journey. I believe I will go to bed. Don't forget to put the fireguard back."

"You are angry with me," Dragan said.

She paused, wrestling with some uncomfortable feeling that seemed to have no name. "You are not...you are not *yourself*, Dragan." *And I will not leave you here alone.*

He frowned up at her though, interestingly, he did not dispute her statement. Leaving him to finish his tea, she prepared for bed. She should have slept as soon as her head touched the pillow, but she did not. She was far too wound up, like a spring, her mind jumping from the poisoned fiancée to her discovery of Dragan asleep at the castle and her sighting of the couple embracing there when she first arrived.

Dragan was not telling her everything. Dragan was *not* himself.

She had left the bedchamber door ajar, so eventually, she heard him move the fireguard back in place and walk across to the bedchamber. The familiar sounds of his undressing and washing soothed her as nothing else since she had arrived.

He slid naked between the sheets, as he always did, and leaned over her. Butterfly light, he smoothed a strand of hair off her face and brushed his lips against her temple. Then he lay down with his arm across her body, as he always did when he slept.

She tried to be relieved that he did not make love to her. But she was not, for Dragan was a very physical man. But then, he was also a considerate man, and she had claimed to be tired. For the first time ever, she had no idea what either of them needed.

Exhausted, she fell asleep at last. Apparently, so did he. For at some point, she turned over, only half-awake, and sighed with pleasure to find her large, warm husband naked in her arms. Half-asleep, their bodies spoke for them, and by the time she was fully awake, things had progressed too far to draw back or even to want to. Urgent, silent passion swept her up, carrying her from clamoring arousal to delight and to joy.

Afterward, he held her, murmuring words of love both sweet and wicked, and she clung to him, smiling as she fell at last into much more contented and satisfied sleep.

⇶⥤⥢⬴

SHE WOKE, INEVITABLY, to Alexander crying for his breakfast. But it was Dragan who brought the baby to her. Apparently, morning coffee had been left in the sitting room, for he came back to bed with two cups and sprawled against the pillows beside her to drink it.

He said nothing about her leaving again, which was as well, for she had no intention of going without a very, very good reason.

"Everyone will be at breakfast," Dragan told her. "Are you ready to meet them all?"

"I am. Who is all?"

"Lord Cathlinn, imperious old martinet, and his dotty spinster sister, Miss Cathlinn. Then there is Robert, the heir, who is rather larger than life, and his wife Claire."

"I met Claire last night. She is very beautiful. And blunt."

"Deliberately so, I suspect. And then there is my friend Richard."

"The bereaved fiancé. Who else?"

"Apart from the servants, no one else."

"From your manner, I assumed there were hordes of them."

"Trust me, those are enough."

"And one of them poisoned Richard's fiancée?"

"Unless it was one of the servants—who all know where the rat poison is and who would have access to all the food and drink prepared in the kitchen."

"Only, why would a servant kill a visitor? What of the victim's own maid? Who claims her mistress took arsenic for her complexion?"

"She showed me the tin and the tiny quantities involved. Even if April forgot and took a double dose, two days running, it would not have been enough to kill her. Though I can't say it was good for her to be taking it at all. The idiocies of vanity." He bent and swiped Alexander off the floor, much to the baby's delight, and they marched off to breakfast *en famille*.

When they arrived in the breakfast parlor, only two men occupied the table, and they appeared to be arguing, although they broke off immediately and rose to their feet, smiling.

"Griz, allow me to present Robert, Master of Cathlinn, and Mr. Richard Cathlinn. Gentlemen, my wife, Lady Grizelda Tisza, and our son, Alexander."

The elder Mr. Cathlinn, who bore the Scottish traditional courtesy title of the heir to a barony, Master, was a large, twinkly eyed gentleman in his mid-thirties, with an impressive mane of auburn hair and luxuriant mustaches. His brother shared the same coloring but was clean shaven, his eyes more thoughtful than constantly laughing at the world, which was the impression Griz got of Robert Cathlinn.

"Lady Grizelda, your humble servant," Robert pronounced, bowing over her hand. "You are most welcome to Cathlinn House. I'm only sorry I was not on hand to greet you."

"Neither was her husband," Richard said dryly. "She had to fetch him home at some ungodly hour. Must do better, Tizsa."

Griz laughed. "If half-past ten is ungodly, sir, I shall ensure we are all tucked up by nine tonight."

"And you are Alexander, are you?" Robert offered the baby his finger. Alexander took it in both hands for a closer inspection, and then tugged it toward his mouth. Robert laughed.

"Yes, it's a baby, Robert," came a sardonic female voice from the door. "Do let poor Mrs. Tizsa put it down. The servants dug out a highchair, Dragan, so he shan't be parted from his mama."

Claire Cathlinn sailed languidly into the room while Griz, with a murmured, "Good morning, Mrs. Cathlinn," settled Alexander into the highchair.

Dragan held the chair beside it for Griz and went to the sideboard, where Mrs. Cathlinn smiled up at him.

"Did you get in trouble for being absent without leave?" she asked in a low voice that Griz was not, presumably meant to hear, although Robert cast his wife an irritated glance.

It seemed everyone knew Dragan had not been in the house when Griz arrived, yet nobody had told her. Or perhaps they had merely been seen returning from the castle. She did not sense any direct hostility from Claire Cathlinn, although the woman was definitely flirting with Dragan. And deliberately using his Christian name while sticking rigidly to Grizelda's proper title, Mrs. Tizsa, even though most people—including Robert—addressed her as Lady Grizelda, her courtesy title as the daughter of a duke. Claire was distinguishing between them too obviously. Which was interesting more than annoying, especially after the sweet and passionate nighttime interlude.

"I fell asleep in the cold, which was trouble enough," Dragan said easily. He turned, placing a plate of Griz's favorite breakfast foods in front of her, before returning to the sideboard to fetch his own.

Griz cut off a toast crust and gave it to Alexander, who grinned at it.

Dragan sat opposite them, just as their host appeared with a lady fluttering in front of him. Everyone stood up again—except Alexander—and Griz was introduced to Lord Cathlinn and his sister.

"Very pleased to meet you," Lord Cathlinn growled, bowing jerkily before stomping off to the sideboard. "Know your father."

"Such a distinguished man, the duke," Miss Cathlinn said dreamily.

"Though quite high in the instep. I danced with him once. Are you like him? I suppose not since you married a foreigner."

"Aunt!" Richard protested while both his brother and sister-in-law snorted with laughter.

"Oh, I'm not high-in-the-instep at all, ma'am," Griz said amiably.

"She is our guest, is she not?" Claire pointed out, but the older lady clearly had meant no harm and was now flustered and apologetic.

"Oh, dear, that came out quite wrongly! It often does with me, you know. And we are very glad to welcome Mr. Tizsa. The Hungarians, you know, are quite the heroes for the gallant way they tried to throw off the emperor's oppression." She leaned closer and all but winked. "And *such* a handsome man!"

"For God's sake, Marie, come and get breakfast," Lord Cathlinn snapped.

Everyone sat down. Griz met Dragan's gaze, and his eyebrows whipped up and then down again quite speakingly. Like her, it seemed, he did not know whether to be amused or irritated with their hosts.

"So, you have already been across to the castle?" Robert Cathlinn said to her. "Not much of it left, sadly, but quite picturesque. It's not really safe, either, so beware. Stones fall down all the time."

"You should fence it off," Richard said.

"But then where would the local lovers go?" Claire said mildly.

"That's a myth anyway," Richard said dismissively. "Courting couples are afraid to go there because it's haunted."

"Oh, by whom?" Griz asked with a manufactured shiver of chilled delight. "How wonderful that you have a ghost."

"Ghosts, plural," Robert said, watching her.

"But the one most often seen is Aileen Cathlinn," Richard added. "Who died a hundred years ago of a broken heart."

Griz let her eyes widen. "Oh dear, do people really die of broken hearts?"

"Well, they have to die of something," Claire drawled. "And if they have a broken heart at the time, the diagnosis is simple. Though I doubt our resident physician would agree."

"Grief can induce melancholia," Dragan said mildly, "which can lead in many directions. In the case of the ghostly Miss Aileen, I understand her death had a definite physical cause."

"She died of complications from being with child," Claire confided mockingly, "but we have to say it in low voices because of the shame. Her betrothed was a Highlander and that horror of horrors, a Jacobite. Rumor says they trysted by the castle ruins, and that is why she went across to the castle to die. She probably died in her bed, but everyone likes to believe her ghost haunts the castle ruins, still waiting for her Highlander to come for her."

"And what happened to him?" Griz asked.

Claire shrugged. "He died at Culloden."

"What a sad tale," Griz commented.

"And not," Richard said tightly, "why April went to the castle."

"Then why do you think she went?" Dragan asked.

"I told you," Richard retorted. "I think she was lured there."

"If it was by ghosts," his brother said with unexpected gentleness, "they were all in her mind. But if she was waiting for you, I wish you would just tell us and get it over with. No one would think the worse of her. She was going to marry you, after all."

Richard met his brother's gaze, and his lips twisted.

He doubts it, Griz thought suddenly. *And thinks his brother should know why.* She itched to ask questions that would only have been rude at this time, and unlikely to be answered truthfully in any case.

So, as if she had not noticed the moment, she reverted to the previous topic. "I might have seen your ghost," she said with awe. "Just as my carriage was arriving last night. We reached the top of the hill, and I was watching the bats—which are such odd creatures, are they not?—and I saw a silvery lady."

Robert laughed. "You are way ahead of yourself, my lady. It is tomorrow night before the ghosts and demons walk on All Hallows' Eve."

"Around here they are quite small ghosts and demons," Claire said placatingly. "They knock politely on the door and are easily placated with fruit and cakes."

"It is the same at Kelburn," Griz agreed. "I guised, too, when I lived there more as a child."

Claire considered her. "What an odd mixture you are, my lady."

"So my family tells me." Actually, they usually just said *odd*.

"Shall we take Alexander for a walk after breakfast?" Dragan asked her.

"What a good idea." She was suddenly desperate to get out of the house.

"He walks already?" Claire blurted.

Dragan laughed. "No, thank God, but he will crawl soon, we think and get into everything we don't want him to. At the moment, we do the walking for him."

Everyone smiled, and yet Griz had the feeling that Claire was somehow embarrassed or humiliated by her mistake, though she gave no obvious signs.

Griz set down her coffee cup. "I'll fetch what we need from our room," she said. "If you will excuse me?"

All the gentlemen stood up again, and she hurried off, relieved to be out of the room. The dynamic between family members was somehow exhausting. Interesting, but exhausting. She needed to talk to Dragan about it out of their hearing.

She opened the door of the sitting room and halted. A maid she hadn't seen before stood by the sofa, fingering her traveling cloak, though she hastily dropped her hands to her sides as Griz erupted into the room.

"Madam," the maid said with a curtsey.

"Yes?"

"I'm Davidson, madam, Mrs. Cathlinn's maid. Since yours is not with you, she sent me to see if I could help you unpack or dress, or if there was anything else you needed."

It was true most people found it off that a duke's daughter did not have a lady's maid, but it was a mixture of personal choice and financial necessity. Mrs. Cathlinn's woman was tall, angular, and middle-aged, and if her accent was Scottish at all, it was only just. She seemed to be of the most supercilious variety of lady's maid, the kind Griz found most repellant.

"Thank you, but no," Griz said pleasantly. And since she suspected the maid was merely curious on her own account, she added, "I shall thank Mrs. Cathlinn for her thoughtfulness the next time I see her.

"You have a child," the woman said, looking about her as though expecting Alexander to leap out from behind her skirts.

"I do. He is downstairs with his father." Griz considered. Gossiping with upper servants rarely endeared one. And yet servants knew more or less everything that went on in any house, and Griz badly wanted away from this one as soon as possible. Besides, Davidson seemed reluctant to depart.

Griz walked over to pick up her cloak. "You are aware my husband is here to help Mr. Richard Cathlinn over the death of Miss April Weir?"

"Not my place to be aware of any such thing, madam."

"Nonsense," Griz snapped. "I'm sure the lowliest kitchen maid knows all about it. I wanted to ask you, as a more educated and reliable person, what you believe happened to Miss Weir."

Davidson shivered. It looked involuntary. "Ghosts."

"Ghosts," Griz repeated.

"It's what Mr. Richard believes."

"Mr. Richard is a grieving man who has lost his bride-to-be. I would have thought you a sensible woman."

Her chin jutted upward. "I hope I am."

"Then what did happen?"

"No one knows," Davidson intoned.

"Did you like Miss Weir?" Griz asked quickly.

The maid blinked. "Like her? Not my place. She was a modern young lady, from trade, and ambitious. Will there be anything else, madam, or shall I get on?"

"Oh, get on, by all means," Griz said amiably and waited for her to go before she flung on the cloak and collected the baby sling.

CHAPTER THREE

"**D**ID THEY TRYST at the castle of an evening?" Griz asked as she and Dragan set out on their walk. Dragan carried the baby, although Griz wore the sling.

"I don't think so," Dragan replied, turning his footsteps toward the fields to the south. "They wouldn't need to. Everyone retires so early that there would be plenty of opportunities to discreetly visit each other and tryst in warmth and comfort."

"But did they?" Griz pursued.

He glanced at her. "I really don't know, though I would suspect not. She was young, and Richard rather had her on a pedestal. Why do you think it's important?"

"If she was with child, she might not have been at her best. What if she took the arsenic herself?"

Dragan frowned. "From shame? She was about to marry, and it would hardly be the first seventh-month baby."

"But *was* she about to marry him?" Griz speculated. Without her noticing, they had somehow reached the road instead of the fields and crossed now toward the castle. "Some look between the brothers bothers me. Richard seemed to doubt that April would have married him. Perhaps they had already broken the engagement before she realized she carried his baby."

"Or the baby was not Richard's, and he had somehow discovered it," Dragan said thoughtfully. "Although I cannot imagine him murdering anyone, let alone the woman he loved and by such a vile way as arsenic poisoning. And then, if by her own hand or his, why would she come up here to die?"

Griz paused and gazed up at the broken, jagged walls of the keep. "Richard thinks the ghosts lured her. Particularly the lady deprived of her Jacobite husband-to-be. Aileen? Who had also been with child. Perhaps, for April, it was simple fellow-feeling. But whatever the reason she came here, I get the impression all was not happy in her engagement."

"Perhaps, but in fact, the autopsy showed she was *not* pregnant."

"But she could have feared that she was, with much the same effects."

"True." Dragan sighed and, holding Alexander in one arm, took her hand and drew her up the rest of the hill. "There is a danger of falling masonry, so we need to pay attention."

Griz cast constant, wary glances upward. Apart from anything else, the crash of large, falling stones, or any loud, sudden noise, could paralyze Dragan, throwing his mind back into the hell of battle.

He said, "I suspect your impression is correct. From what I hear, she was a flirtatious girl, and Richard did not like it."

"Did she flirt with someone here?"

"I doubt she would lower herself with the footmen, which leaves only Richard's father and brother."

"The brother who is the heir and not a little flirtatious himself."

"The married brother," Dragan pointed out.

"How long have they been married?" Griz asked.

He shrugged. "Five years or so, I believe."

"And no children. It bothers her, though she will never admit it."

"Claire is also flirtatious. But I cannot see her poisoning a younger woman who dares flirt with her husband."

"Perhaps the poison was meant for Claire," Griz said, sitting down on a rock from where she could see across the fields to the distant city of Glasgow in the north, and Cathlinn House closer to the east. A river, perhaps a tributary of the more majestic Clyde, meandered through Cathlinn land, and a village sprawled along its banks.

"With April as would-be murderer instead of victim?" Dragan murmured, sprawling at her feet and sitting the baby beside his feet. "Only she somehow drank the wrong tea or whatever?"

"Would you taste it in tea?"

"You wouldn't really taste it in anything," he said grimly. "Which is why rats will eat it so happily, and the reason I want you to leave."

"We have already agreed that another death in this house from arsenic poisoning would bring the authorities in droves and accompanying scandal."

"Griz, there are other poisons in the world."

A memory flashed through her brain. "You smelled the tea last night. You tasted it very gingerly."

"Hardly infallible," he said ruefully. "But the best I can do with anything not eaten by the rest of the household."

"Then we shall eat like birds with delicate stomachs. And buy pies in the village to consume in private later."

A breath of laughter escaped him. "Not such a bad idea." He caught Alexander's hand to prevent him stuffing brown and gold leaves into his mouth, then brushed off the dirt before standing and swinging the baby back up into his arms. "Come, then, to the village."

As she stood, something caught the corner of her eye, and she turned back frowning. No one was there, but just for an instant, she had imagined a slender, long-fingered hand trailing possessively over Dragan's shoulder and vanishing into the nearby stones.

She shivered. "This place *is* eerie. Do you feel it?"

His lips twisted. "I try not to. I am a man of science and logic, not fairy tales and the supernatural."

"Do you never think there are reasons behind those old tales and beliefs?"

"Yes, enabling the control of their social superiors."

"Stop being a radical and just be human. Supernatural beliefs are not limited by class or education. There is an upper-class fashion for mediums, you know, who let the dead talk through them."

"They are charlatans."

"Yes, but again the beliefs that allow them to be accepted are older than Christianity, as old as time."

"It doesn't make them right," Dragan insisted as they walked down the other side of the hill toward the river and the village. "People just made up stories to try to explain the natural world around them. They still do."

Griz looked up at him. "So, if I saw a woman in your arms last night, it is my mind making sense of a ghostly lover?"

He met her gaze, watchful, as unreadable as he had been when she had first met him. "You were the only woman in my arms last night."

She shivered and glanced back over her shoulder. What was left of the castle glared back at her, as though determined to outlast her despite its ruined state.

"And if you did not believe that," he said quietly, "you would already be halfway back to Kelburn with Alexander."

"Or at least be rummaging below stairs for the rat poison."

"Then you think the murder is about infidelity?"

"That house seethes with emotion," Griz said. "Even the family cannot abide it, which is no doubt why they retire each night before most children have heard their bedtime story." She frowned. "Or *do* they retire? Did it give Richard time to visit his soon-to-be bride? Or the bride to visit elsewhere? And what is the story of Claire and Robert? Why do they not have children?"

"No one speaks of it. It happens sometimes, despite a couple's best efforts. While other times children can be born from a mere moment's inattention."

"She likes you," Griz said reluctantly. "Claire."

"I think she likes you, too."

"I suspect she has not made up her mind about the inconvenience that is me." But Dragan... Dragan was a startlingly handsome man. Some had called him gorgeous in Griz's hearing, though there was so much more to him that she sometimes forgot he attracted notice for his looks alone. For never, since they had agreed to marry, had she doubted him. She was not beautiful, but he found her so. They were soul mates on some profound level she did not need to analyze, and in that time, she had never once been jealous of another woman.

Until she had come here and seen the couple by the castle, and Claire Cathlinn with her sultry eyes and subtle belittling of Dragan's wife. Did she do that to all women? Had she done it to poor April Weir?

>>>*<<<

RAIN CAME ON as they were returning to Cathlinn House and looked likely to stay on for the rest of the afternoon. Although the Cathlinns seemed to feel no obligation to entertain their guests, whatever the weather, Richard did join them for a time in the library.

He glanced worriedly at Alexander, enjoying his afternoon nap on the sofa beside Griz.

"Oh, don't worry," Dragan said. "Once asleep, an artillery bombardment couldn't wake him before he is ready."

"Strange having a baby in the house," Richard remarked, sitting down in the chair next to Dragan's.

"I'm just relieved he seems to have recovered his good nature," Griz said. "He screamed for most of the journey north from London, and for three of my four days at Kelburn."

Richard smiled crookedly. "Is that what compelled you to answer my plea, Tizsa?"

"On the contrary. It almost compelled me to refuse," Dragan said mildly.

"Dragan has been telling me about Miss Weir," Griz said. "I am so sorry."

He bowed his head. "We are all sorry."

"What do *you* think happened?" Griz asked.

He shrugged. "That she took substances she should not, merely to look even more beautiful. And her heart was not up to the effects."

"Dragan thinks she had not taken enough or for long enough to have done herself that degree of ill."

Richard cast a less than friendly glance at Dragan. "Dragan is not infallible."

"No, but he is knowledgeable and dispassionate in such matters."

"My lady, do you expect me to be dispassionate about the tragic death of my fiancée?"

"No," Griz replied. "That is why you have Dragan and me to help."

Richard's hand, clawing through his hair, tightened.

Griz said gently, "You do *want* to know what happened to her, don't you?"

"Would you?" he retorted.

"Yes. It might be more comfortable to believe her death was a tragic accident, depriving you of your happy future together, but—"

"But it would never have been that, would it?" Richard interrupted. "A happy future in this house?"

"She would have brought you the means to live elsewhere," Dragan pointed out.

"She liked the idea of being lady of the manor. A traditional old manor like Cathlinn."

"But she would never have been that, would she?"

Richard shrugged. "Robert has no heirs."

"You think she preferred your brother?" Griz asked brutally.

Richard sneered. "Don't you?"

"Right now, yes," Griz replied. "But then, I thank God I am married to Dragan."

Richard flushed. "You should," he said gruffly. "He is a good friend, and I apologize to you both for my rudeness."

"I apologize for my intrusive questions," Griz returned at once. "But Dragan and I help each other to solve puzzles, sometimes tragic ones like yours. Did you love Miss Weir?"

He nodded once.

"And she loved you?"

He groaned. "I don't know. I truly don't. I thought she did. I was the happiest of men when she accepted me, and then, almost as soon as she came to Cathlinn House, she seemed to fall under Robert's damned spell. Pardon my language, my lady."

"Would anyone in this house wish her dead?" Griz asked, as gently as she could.

His eyes were harrowed as they lifted to hers. "If Tizsa is right, then somebody more than wished it. But dash it, no one would do such a thing!"

"Servants?" Griz asked.

Richard waved one dismissive hand. "Tizsa has already been through this with me. And spoken to the servants. They have all been with us for years—generations of them in some cases. Our honor is theirs, so no, I cannot imagine any of them guilty of such a thing either. Tizsa, a walk in the rain?"

Dragan glanced at Griz, who nodded infinitesimally, and the men went off on their walk. Griz picked up her book and remained beside the sleeping baby to see if anyone else would disturb her.

She did not have long to wait before Claire wandered in. She showed no surprise at finding Griz there, so it must have been deliberate. She walked over and gazed down at the baby in silence for several moments. Although her expression was hard to read, it did not appear to be malevolent.

"Will he wake if we talk?" she murmured.

"Lord, no. My brothers' singing doesn't even disturb him, and that racket would wake the dead. Sorry, that was careless."

"Was it?" Claire asked wryly, and rightly, for Griz had indeed been looking for reaction. Claire sank elegantly onto the chair Dragan had recently vacated. "Dragan says you can help him find out what happened to April. I find that hard to believe, too."

"Why? Neither of us are stupid women."

"No, which is why I could see through your little act at breakfast."

"That was largely for the men," Griz admitted.

Claire's lips quirked. "I'm sure I shouldn't like you ei…"

"Either?" Griz suggested when she tailed off. "Did you not like April?"

Claire shrugged. "No. She was vapid, ambitious, silly, *young.*"

"And not good enough for a Cathlinn?"

"My dear, *I* am not good enough for a Cathlinn. Robert married me on a whim and is stuck with me."

"Did April flirt with Robert?"

"She flirted with every male who came near her, and they were all flattered."

"Why do you think she chose Richard from all her admirers, then?"

Claire did her the courtesy of thinking about it. Or seeming to. "I suppose you are not seeing Richard at his best. But he is quite charming under normal circumstances. And devoted."

"To you?" Griz asked, because bluntness appeared to work better with this woman.

Claire laughed. "My dear, one Cathlinn is too much for me. Richard was devoted to April, and to his family."

Something sparked in Griz's brain. "Do you think…was April somehow a *threat* to the family?"

"I don't see how, apart from making Richard miserable. To be honest, it would have been better for all of us if Richard had married her and gone to live elsewhere."

Griz frowned. "But would she have lived elsewhere? Did she not look forward to being…if not *the* lady of Cathlinn, at least *a* lady of Cathlinn?"

Claire hesitated. "Look. I'm sure she imagined she would love to be Robert's wife instead of Richard's and Lady Cathlinn one day. But the reality is, Robert would never divorce me. His father would not allow it."

Although a sardonic smile accompanied this startling statement, she could not quite hide the bitterness. All was not well in her marriage. But Griz doubted she could force any further confidences on that topic. She doubted it was relevant, although there was so much in this house and its environs that did not appear to be relevant.

"Do you believe in ghosts, Mrs. Cathlinn?" she asked, the words spilling out before she had properly considered them.

"That again?" Claire said, amused. "No, of course I don't."

"Claire's ancestry is hardly conducive to such sightings," Robert said, wandering into the room. He sounded more amused than disparaging. "Her family is English. But then, it's largely the servants who see ghosts, so you may judge whether that is due to Celtic ancestry or mere ignorance." He paused, catching sight of the baby, and his face softened. Was that hint of regret in his eyes because he had no children of his own yet? His eyes lifted to Grizelda's. "You must be a very proud mother."

Claire stood up and walked out of the room.

"I am," Griz replied, dragging her frowning gaze from Claire's back to Robert's face. "But was it kind to point it out to your wife?"

"Claire goes where and when she likes. She is not so sensitive to my remarks as you appear to be." He moved to lean on the arm of the sofa right next to her and gave her the full benefit of his twinkling smile.

Griz had no difficulty withstanding it. She was, after all, married to Dragan Tizsa. "I think we both know that is a lie."

His eyebrows flew up. "You don't pull your punches, do you, my lady?"

"It can be too easy to miss what is right under one's own eyes. I hope someone would tell me."

"What, trouble in my lady's own marriage?" he teased, only just on the right side of mockery. "How can this be? Of course, you are a relatively new mother, daughter of a wealthy duke, and Tizsa is a romantic refugee pauper with a heroic background and more masculine beauty than any one man has a right to. It must be difficult for you, too."

"Being so plain that I was clearly only married for my father's wealth," she said affably. "What did you think of April Weir?"

A flash of something that might have been admiration lit his eyes for an instant before he shrugged. "She was pretty, empty-headed, and not good enough for my brother."

"Even though he loved her?"

"I could tolerate empty-headedness," he said mildly, "if she had loved him."

"You think she did not?"

"She...flirted too intensely with me."

Griz caught her breath. "You were testing her? Dragan thought you liked her."

"I might have liked her in my bed ten years ago if she was a lady of easy virtue. Since she was of respectable family and my brother's fiancée, I never considered it. Shocked?"

"Yes, but not by that foolish little speech." Griz rose and picked up the sleeping baby before staring up at Robert Cathlinn. "Do any of you actually *care* how that girl died? Or even that she *is* dead, let alone which of you is responsible? No, don't answer that. It's plain enough. Excuse me."

Before she reached the door, which had remained open throughout, he stood in front of her, as though being polite, though she was forced to halt in her grand exit.

"I am honoring you with the truth," he said impatiently. "Because whatever happened to her, none of my family is responsible."

Directly or indirectly?

For once, the twinkle was not present, and he sounded very certain.

She inclined her head. "I am very glad to hear it. The baby is waking, sir, and I will not vouch for the pleasure of that experience."

He stood aside, and she left the room, walking so quickly across the hall to the staircase that Alexander did indeed wake up. By the time they reached the half-landing, he had realized how hungry he was, and Griz felt vindictively glad to let him exercise his powerful little lungs in a few moments of screaming that must have reached every corner of the house.

CHAPTER FOUR

A LEXANDER WAS FED and changed and jumping up and down on his bottom trying to catch his spinning top when the maid Jeanie appeared with a tray.

"I brought you some tea and scones, my lady," she said cheerfully.

"Thank you," Griz replied from her position on the floor. She spun the top again. "Will you leave it on the taller table, please? Just in case he lunges for it."

"Of course!" Jeanie all but dumped the tray in her hurry to admire Alexander. "What a happy wee man he is. Shall I pour the tea for you, ma'am?"

"No, that's fine, thank you."

"Mr. Tizsa's just back from his walk with Mr. Richard," the maid reported, still beaming at Alexander. "I expect he'll be up in a minute to change. Still raining. Hope it's better for the guisers tomorrow evening."

"Ah, yes, Halloween," Griz said, extracting the top from Alexander, who was sucking on the end of it. She spun it for him again, and he bounced with excitement. "When all the ghosts and demons rise up and the children disguise themselves so they can walk among them with safety."

"So they say," Jeanie grinned.

"You don't believe it?"

"Of course not," Jeanie scoffed. "It's just fun."

"Then you've never seen ghosts over at the castle?"

"No!" She looked up at the window, though, through which she could probably see the castle, and shivered. "I don't like it, mind. Weird place. Always was, but I never saw a ghost there or anywhere else. Some of the others claim they have, but I reckon they just say so for attention."

She glanced at Alexander again and smiled. "Lovely wee boy," she told Griz, "but I'd better get back to work."

"Thanks for the tea."

When the maid had closed the door, Griz stood and walked to the teapot with one eye on Alexander. Without looking at it, she picked up the pot—and paused for several seconds before she laid it back down again.

Blinking, she went and retrieved Alexander who seemed to have bottom-bumped most of the way to the door. She had just picked him up when the door opened and a rather wet Dragan strode in, shaking his head. As water flew off him, Alexander chortled and grabbed at his face.

Dragan blinked, clearly surprised to find them quite so close.

"Miss me?" he asked in amusement.

"Madly. Dragan, what did you eat or drink last night?" She plonked Alexander back on the floor and spun the top before going to help her husband wrestle himself out of his wet coat.

"I'm not poisoned," he said mildly.

"No, but you should never have fallen asleep in the cold, should you? Not unless you were dead drunk. Or drugged."

He watched her as she hung his coat up and went to find him dry clothes. "Drugged," he repeated, and she knew the notion was not new to him.

"You said yourself there is more than arsenic that could be put in tea. Or anything else."

He sighed. "To be honest, I don't really remember going over to the castle. And I had such strange dreams."

"Dragan." She almost threw his clothes at him. "Why did you not tell me?"

"Because I was worried I had over-indulged. Because I didn't want to concern you. Because I was scared for you."

"Have we not always been beyond that kind of secrecy?" she demanded.

He nodded, frowning, as though he didn't understand it. Then he rubbed his forehead, just over his eyes. "I don't like this place, Griz. Even Richard is different here, though I suppose he has the excuse of a murdered fiancée. But someone poisoned April Weir, and I can see no reason for it. No one has anything to gain by it."

"Perhaps they did, and they drugged you to make you give up trying to find out what."

Dragan changed his clothes in silence, then went to the teapot and poured two half cups. He sniffed each of them. "I don't know why I'm bothering, if they managed to drug me with something already. A mouthful only, Griz. The same for anything that is served only to you or me."

She nodded and went to the cupboard beneath the window and brought out the apple tart they had bought in the village. Cutting two slices, she put them on a plate and returned the pie to its hiding place. Sitting together on the sofa, they ate in silence.

Then he said, "I've wasted time not acknowledging this before. I should have been working out who could have contaminated..."

"Contaminated what?" she asked as he broke off. "When did you start feeling sleepy last night?"

"After dinner. I went with Richard to his rooms, and we talked about the arsenic in April's stomach. My mind was clear enough then, though I was annoyed with Richard for refusing to believe the evidence. We had a couple of glasses of brandy."

"Served from the same bottle? Was Richard affected?"

"I don't know," Dragan said slowly. "His lordship keeps the brandy strictly rationed. A glass after dinner and then another delivered to the gentlemen's rooms. The talkative maid, Jeanie, brought it to Richard's. And then, when Richard rang, she brought another. The first glasses will have lain around in the hallways as she distributed them to all the gentlemen, so anyone passing could have drugged them."

"But then, how could the perpetrator be sure you would get the correct glass? And if he or she indiscriminately drugged them all, several people, especially Richard, would have been affected, too?"

"Maybe they were, although no one has told me so."

Griz looked at him and said what they were both thinking. "Richard is the obvious suspect. Only he would have known which glass was yours. And he was closest to April."

"And eager to go with the theory that the arsenic in her stomach was only cosmetic and that her weak heart killed her."

Griz nodded. "He could have enticed her to the castle so that there was no one to help her when she was taken ill. Or even administered the poison there?"

"Possible. The trouble is, I can't actually imagine him behaving in such a way. Railing and shouting, yes, but poisoning? Hard to believe. One of the many other things that bothers me is Claire discovered April missing from her bed. What was Claire doing there after midnight?"

"Did you ask her?"

"Yes. She said she knew April never retired early and went to talk to her."

"What about?"

"She told me she had no particular reason, implying she was only looking for company."

Griz said, "She didn't care for April. If she sought her out, it was probably to tell her off for flirting with her husband."

"Or to poison her," Dragan said grimly.

"Is she so jealous of her husband's attention that she would do such a thing?"

"I have no idea. She would have to be pretty unhinged. But then, so would anyone else. She gives no sign of being that unhappy."

"She *is* unhappy, though."

Dragan's lips quirked, and he nudged her with his shoulder. "This is why I needed you. These people baffle me."

Griz leaned against his shoulder, watching Alexander push the spinning top about and bounce after it. "And they have gone from wanting you to solve the puzzle to drugging you so that you can't. That doesn't make sense either."

"It does if the person who invited me is not the poisoner."

"True."

Dragan took the empty plate and rose restlessly to his feet. "We do not even know when she went to the castle that night. No one admits to seeing her go, or to seeing her at all after dinner."

"Not even Richard?" she asked.

He put the plate with the others on the tray and began to pace. "They all had tea together in the drawing room after dinner, then Richard accompanied April upstairs and said goodnight at her door."

"Do we know that he left her there?"

"We know he came back to the drawing room to finish his own tea, for every member of his family and several servants saw him do so."

"Or said they did," Griz said thoughtfully. "They might lie to cover for him."

"They might. But it makes little difference because they all retired very shortly after to their own rooms. Anyone could have visited April after that and not been seen."

"Including Claire," Griz mused, "earlier than she claimed. Do she and her husband share rooms?"

"Connecting rooms. I understand the relationship is volatile. They did not spend the evening together but claim to have heard each other moving around."

Griz scowled. "Nothing is certain, nothing is provable. Everyone could be lying."

"And that is before you even start on the servants."

"What a pity we cannot speak to April's own maid."

"I spoke to her," Dragan said. "April dismissed her almost as soon as she retired. She got the maid to unlace her and then sent her away. She did not ring for anything during the evening. And she was found in her night clothes beneath a cloak."

Griz rose and scooped up the baby who was getting too close to the door. He chortled and threw his little arms around her neck, making her smile and ache at the same time. She had been so lucky in her life. But then, she had not looked for marriage. It had found her in the shape of Dragan. April had not waited at all. She seemed to have had no other interest except marrying well, a type of young lady with which Griz was only too familiar.

Carrying the baby, she walked over to the window to join Dragan. "Would April have gone to an assignation in her night clothes? Surely, she was always well dressed in public."

Dragan turned his gaze from the ruined castle to Griz. "She could have been drugged as I was and taken to the castle. And poisoned there." He waved one impatient hand. "But it is all speculation. There is no evidence."

"What of the household rat poison?" she said suddenly. "Is it where it should be?"

"Yes, it was the first thing I looked at. It's kept outside in a garden shed, which is locked. Though there are several keys. And no one could say how much, if any, was missing."

Griz shivered. "I feel...unsafe here. I feel everyone is unsafe."

"You and Alexander should return to Kelburn first thing tomorrow."

"I won't leave you here."

A loud knock on the door startled them both.

"Enter," Dragan called, and Robert Cathlinn stuck his head around the door.

"Forgive the intrusion," he said cheerfully. "Tizsa, come and play billiards before dinner. You're on my team."

She could see Dragan's refusal on his face because he feared for her left alone. As she feared for him. But if they were to do any good, they could not skulk here alone.

"Go on, Dragan," she urged. "I have some things to do before I change for dinner."

He met her gaze, then his frown smoothed, and he kissed her cheek, and departed.

While she played with the baby, she made intermittent lists of suspects and motives and alibis, for both the murder of April Weir and the drugging of Dragan.

≫≫≪≪

ON THEIR WAY down to dinner that evening, Griz paused to examine some of the family portraits hung in the upstairs hall and the staircase. One or two were as old as the seventeenth century, though it was the eighteenth-century ones that truly interested her.

She stopped before a lady in a powdered wig, with rouged cheeks and a patch at the corner of her mouth. "Do you suppose this is the Jacobite ghost lady?"

"Lord, no," said another voice before Dragan would speak. "She's around here out of the way."

Lord Cathlinn's sister, blinking amiably, beckoned them to the passage she had just emerged from. Daylight was fading, and no lamps had yet been lit.

"There she is," Miss Cathlinn said, pointing to a portrait of a very young lady. Her hair was unpowdered, her skin natural, and her smile wide. Her blue eyes danced very like Robert's. "Aileen Cathlinn. Tragic, really. She should have married Kenneth MacDonald of Dunmore, but when the clans rose, her family wouldn't hear of her going north. They kept her here, presumably until they saw which way the wind would blow."

"She even has a tragic face," Griz mused. "Even when she smiles..." And there was something familiar about her. More than Robert's eyes. Something in the angle of her head, the slope of her shoulders.

A shiver ran down Griz's spine, perhaps because Miss Cathlinn stood so close behind her. Dragan shifted as though by accident, and the old lady moved away.

Griz considered the way she—and presumably everyone else in the house—thought of Miss Cathlinn. A half-dotty old spinster, vague, harmless, invisible. But...

"You see everything that goes on in this house, don't you, Miss Cathlinn," Griz said amiably as they walked back toward the staircase.

The old lady smiled sweetly. "I like to understand the past."

"And the present, I suspect."

Civilly, Dragan offered Miss Cathlinn his arm, and she took it gratefully to descend the stairs.

"Well, I am not blind," she said.

"What do you really think happened to April Weir?" Dragan asked her.

Miss Cathlinn smiled. "Whatever his lordship says happened to her."

That seemed to flummox Dragan, but Griz, the duke's daughter, was made of sterner stuff.

"Come, madam," she said, "that will not do! You are a wise lady and well aware your opinion counts more than most. Whether or not you choose to air it."

"And I don't. Except to say none of this family would have hurt that poor, troublesome girl. And I will never believe otherwise, whatever dirt you imagine you are digging up, young man."

She gave Dragan's sleeve a little shake as she spoke.

"The truth is not dirt, ma'am," Dragan said seriously. "It is necessary."

She nodded, but her mind seemed to have moved on for she said, "Tonight is not Halloween, is it? Tomorrow, of course. I am quite looking forward to the chaos!"

It struck Griz then, that there seemed no sane reason to have killed April Weir. And so, perhaps they were looking for someone who was not quite sane either. Did dotty and sincere-sounding old ladies count as not quite sane?

DINNER WAS A civilized meal, with intelligent conversation, although controlled by Lord Cathlinn and Claire, so that it never strayed from the impersonal. The food was adequate, if plain for an aristocratic family entertaining guests, and the wine was of good quality if not quantity. In all, it was hardly the generous hospitality one expected in Scotland.

Though of course, Dragan was poking his nose into their business, and they didn't like it. It was far more convenient to believe that April had died of a weak heart rather than by poison administered by one of their household.

Griz, who felt she could cut the tension with a knife, was relieved when Claire declared it time for the ladies to withdraw. She more than half expected her hostess to buttonhole her and ask for the date of her departure.

However, Claire surprised her again. "Is little Alexander still awake?" she asked as they walked to the drawing room. "Bring him down if you like."

"Are you sure? I'm afraid I stole the services of one of your maids to sit with him."

"Davidson, I hope. She seemed very keen to be considered for such duties."

"No, I asked Jeanie. Although I thank you for offering your own maid this morning."

She looked as if she had forgotten about that but said only, "Well, don't disturb the little one, but if he's up to it, I'm sure we'd all enjoy the fun."

Alexander, bless him, would also be an excuse to retire early. Not that early retirement seemed to be a problem in this house. Griz hurried upstairs and found both Jeanie and Davidson sitting on the sofa, gushing over the baby who sat between them, gnawing on his teething toy and grinning around it.

Davidson, her smile fixed, stood at once and said, "The girl is not qualified to look after an infant. Please call upon me in the future."

"Thank you, I will, if it does not interfere with your duties to Mrs. Cathlinn. And Jeanie has been most helpful. Thank you, Jeanie."

Alexander stretched up his arms to Griz, and she swept him up along with a shawl and his spinning top. "I'm taking him down to the drawing room, so you may both return to your duties with my thanks."

It struck her as she carried Alexander downstairs, that two maids were, in fact, safer than one, for while she could not imagine either of them harming a baby, it was perfectly possible one of them had killed April Weir and drugged Dragan.

Maybe Dragan was right. Maybe she should take Alexander away from here in the morning.

For the next half hour, Alexander happily entertained the household, laughing at the spinning top, chewing it occasionally, bouncing on his bottom and investigating everything that caught his fancy, from

Miss Cathlinn's old-fashioned shoe buckles to Claire's embroidered gown. The gentlemen joined them after only ten minutes or so, and to her surprise, none of them objected to the baby's presence either. Robert seemed quite taken with him, and even his lordship smiled benignly.

"Pleasant to have a baby about the place again," he said bluffly, then glowered. "And no, Claire, that is not a snipe at you."

"I didn't suppose it was," she replied mildly. "Shall I hold him for you, Mrs. Tizsa? And let you drink your tea?"

The tea all came out of the same pot, the same sugar bowl, and cream jug, so Griz felt safe enough, although she had watched the servants who brought it, and how everyone had collected their own cup and saucer from Claire. No other beverage was offered or requested.

Lord Cathlinn was the first to retire, with a curt nod and a "Good night, all. Sleep well."

Through the chorus of polite replies, Griz recalled his sister's words, that she thought whatever his lordship told her to. Even over his sons, his word appeared to be law. How much power did he imagine this gave him? If April had not obeyed him, or shown a desire to upset one son for the sake of the other, how far would he be prepared to go?

Poisoning, however, did not seem much in his style. Although she knew him no better than anyone else in the house.

When Alexander began to rub his eyes and get slightly fractious, Dragan took him from Claire. "Shall we take him up to bed?"

"Yes, it seems to be time."

Robert was already heading for the door.

As Griz followed him, Dragan and Alexander, Richard said, "Nightcap, Tizsa?"

"Not tonight," Dragan said easily, "All the coming and going disturbs the little tyrant sometimes. Good night."

CHAPTER FIVE

"HE MIGHT TELL you things we need to know," Griz observed, while giving Alexander his final feed of the day in their bedchamber.

"He might," Dragan agreed from the window seat, where he regarded her and the baby. "But I doubt he has anything to add. I certainly don't want to be drinking drugged brandy again, whether at his hand or someone else's."

"Why are you smiling about it?"

"I'm not. I'm smiling at you and our son. I like to watch you feeding him. Actually, I just like to watch you."

Her body flushed in response. She really, really wanted away from Cathlinn House. This was not a fun puzzle to solve, not an adventure that she could race through hand-in-hand with Dragan.

"We need to finish this," she said low. Laying the half-asleep Alexander on the bed, she changed him, cuddled him, and laid him in his cot. Thankfully, he seemed to be in no teething pain, although no tooth had yet appeared.

"Finish it how?" Dragan asked, leading her through to the sitting room. "We have no evidence, no clue as to who is responsible. I want you away from here, too, but it goes against the grain to let a killer—"

A knock on the door heralded Jeanie with a glass of brandy. "Nightcap, sir," she said cheerfully. "Can I fetch you anything, my lady?"

"No, thank you."

Dragan took the glass from her tray with a word of thanks. When she had gone, he poured it into a vase of wilting flowers, took a flask from his pocket, and held it out to Griz.

With a breath of laughter, she took it and drank. "It's water!"

"Straight from the pump in the kitchen. The spare flask is full, too. No point in dehydrating ourselves for fear of poison." He sat beside her on the window seat and accepted the flask back from her. He took a sizeable drink and screwed the top back on, while Griz mulled over a new idea.

"We have no evidence *yet*," she corrected, harking back to his earlier words.

His gaze flew to hers. "You have a plan?"

"A possible one. If we pretend to have found something, to know how and by whose hand April died, we would draw the attention of the killer."

"My least favorite attention."

"We will appear over-confident and smug, perhaps promise to reveal all after the guisers have been tomorrow evening. The killer will want to silence us."

"And poor Alexander will be left alone in this damned house."

"No, he won't," Griz said eagerly, "because we will look out for each other. We know how this killer works. And we will need to watch the passage and the castle." As she spoke, she glanced through the darkened window to the ruined keep.

The rain seemed to have gone off, but the sky was still cloudy and the night dark. Just for an instant, the black keep seemed whole and square, with crenellations all the way round, and the shadows surrounding it looked like buildings sprawling down the hill to the wall. Then she blinked, and the buildings became no more than the scattering of bushes and trees she was used to. The jagged outline of the ruined keep was clear, even in the darkness.

But there was no time for relief, for a silvery-white figure drifted in front of the old castle, almost like Claire's graceful glide.

Griz shoved her spectacles up her nose and peered. "Dragan!"

"What?" He pressed his nose to the window, gazing where she did. The figure, clearly a woman, wound herself around a tall stone and clung, very still, much as Griz had seen her cling to Dragan last night.

"Who *is* that?" Griz demanded. "She moves like Claire and yet..." The figure turned, as though looking toward the house. Griz could almost imagine she gazed straight at her window. And the face, while familiar, was not Claire's.

"Where?" Dragan demanded.

"Right in front of the ruin. By that tall stone on the left."

Dragan's gaze moved to her. "Griz, there's no one there."

Her heart twisted in sudden fear. Dark, bat-shaped shadows rose against the cloudy sky as she swung around to him. "No one? But I am not seeing things, I am not drugged...am I?"

As Dragan put his arm around her, she stared from his concerned face back to the castle. And saw that he was right. No one was there.

THE FOLLOWING MORNING, Dragan picked up the fed and changed baby and took Grizelda's hand. It struck him that they almost marched across the bedroom and the sitting room, as if they were going into battle. Which, in a way, they were. And some part of him recognized the element of mingled fun and determination which always came with their joint adventures. However, at this moment, he could not shake off a vague sense of anxiety that was almost...ominous.

And yet Griz's plan was good—or would be with a few subtle changes he had no intention of revealing to her until she was forced to agree with them. Last night, she had clung to him, seeking to lose herself in love with an intensity that was beyond her usual delicious passion. Whatever tricks her mind had played on her over the ghostly figure she had imagined in the castle, they had unbalanced her, made her feel unsafe.

Griz was vulnerable. Few people saw that, but Dragan did. It was one of the reasons she sought adventures with him, to overcome, to prove to herself. And Dragan would do everything in his power to protect her.

He had to release her hand to open the door, so he paused for a moment to touch her cheek and kiss her. "It is a good plan."

She nodded, squared her shoulders, and marched through the open door.

Everyone was already in the breakfast parlor when they arrived. So, they said their good mornings, and just like yesterday, Dragan sat Alexander in the highchair, held the seat next to it for his wife, and went to fetch them both breakfast and coffee.

"Thunder in the air, according to Tam Shepherd," Lord Cathlinn said.

Dragan's sense of unease grew. He did not function well in thunderstorms, not since the war.

"Well, that should spoil the guisers' fun," Claire remarked.

"Or increase it," Robert argued. "They can scare each other witless while angry thunder and lightning crashes overhead."

"Expect it will be over by then," Richard said, "if Tam's predicting thunder already."

"We shall have an early meal tonight," Claire said as Dragan finally sat down. "So that we can enjoy the guisers. They are usually quite entertaining."

A manservant and a maid were hovering by the door, perfect conduits to spread the word below stairs, so Dragan began to implement the plan. "Griz and I must thank you all for your kind hospitality at what I know is a very difficult time. We mean to depart tomorrow morning."

"So soon?" Richard said from across the table. He sounded both surprised and chagrined. "Then you have finally accepted the truth of April's tragic death?"

"I believe I *know* the truth of April's tragic death," Dragan corrected. "And I would like to explain it to you and the rest of the household before I leave to speak to the authorities. Perhaps this evening? About nine or ten of the clock?"

"What is wrong with now?" Lord Cathlinn growled.

Dragan did not look at Griz. "I do not wish to spoil my wife's day with the ugly truth."

He was aware that on the other side of the highchair, Grizelda's head turned toward him.

"Even your wife does not know?" Claire asked amused. "I thought you wanted her here to help you?"

"And she has helped me. Her insight has been invaluable in reaching the truth."

"Dragan," Griz said warningly. She knew exactly what he was about.

He smiled at her, aiming to appear the perfectly implacable and slightly superior husband. "No, my dear. You must wait until this evening, too."

"Damned theatrics," Lord Cathlinn uttered, glaring at him. "There is no need to turn this tragedy into some circus for your own entertainment."

"I do not find murder remotely entertaining," Dragan said coldly. "And neither will you."

"THAT WAS NOT the plan," Griz said between her teeth as they walked in the opposite direction to the castle. She was not so much angry as hurt by Dragan's sudden exclusion of her from the plan which had been hers in the first place.

"But you see the sense in it," he argued. "If the killer only has one of us to attack, it makes the threat easier to track."

"And you did not bring this up last night because…?"

"Because you were not thinking quite straight," he said quietly.

"Because I hallucinated?" she snapped.

"This place has you too wound up, Griz. A trick of the eye, of the mind, in line with one's fears or hopes is not so unusual. You know that. But your immediate response is to hurl yourself into the breach to prove you are worthy. You *are* worthy, and for the rest of the day and the evening, I will need your protection."

She frowned up at him in quick understanding. "Especially if it thunders."

He nodded.

Loud and sudden noises were his weakness, a result of his experience in battle. She had seen it utterly debilitate him, and though he was dealing with it better now, she prayed there would be no thunder to distract him today.

"Perhaps there will be no storm," she said, looking up at the cloudy but dry sky. "It does not feel like thunder to me." Not yet.

He changed the subject as they reached the top of another incline. "The locals believe Mary, Queen of Scots, watched the Battle of Langside from here before fleeing to England. Cathlinn disagrees."

"Cathlinn disagrees with everything on principle." She wanted desperately to stay out here all day, with Dragan and Alexander, and never go back to the house. Sadly, that would defeat their entire object. "Shall we walk to the village and buy another pie?"

THE HOURS PASSED uneasily. The very air seemed to grow heavy and ominous, and Griz thought they would be lucky to escape a thunderstorm. She avoided looking at the castle, and yet the figure she had seen there haunted her mind. She even found herself drawn back to the portrait of Aileen Cathlinn.

Griz did not believe in ghosts.

And yet there had been odd incidents during her childhood in Kelburn: a whisper of heavy skirts in a silent, empty passage; a song in her dreams that she could repeat but that no one else knew; shadows of…nothing. Friends that everyone else had called imaginary teased the edges of her memory.

She had forgotten those incidents, dismissed them as the fantasies of a lonely child whose older brothers and sisters had been only too happy to leave her behind. And now she could no longer remember whether any of them had been real or part of a story she had made up.

But last night's ghost had looked real, more real than the painted face in the portrait before her. So had the girl wrapped around Dragan on the night she had arrived. Was the ghost some kind of trick to scare her off, taking Dragan with her? Though if so, why had Dragan not seen the shade, too?

Either way, she had to keep her wits about her, for everyone's sake.

She turned from the portrait and walked toward the stairs. Behind her, she thought she heard a door softly closing, and the hairs on the back of her neck prickled. Everyone, family and staff, would be watching her today, though not as closely as they would watch Dragan, who had set himself up to be murdered.

She descended the staircase and made her way outside by the side door, and around to the stables. The air felt close and heavy now and she feared there would indeed be a thunderstorm.

A few grooms were playing pitch and toss against the wall with farthings and halfpennies, though they stopped at the sight of her and nodded by way of respect.

"Will one of you send my coachman out to me, please?" she asked pleasantly, though as it turned out there was no need, for Ewan emerged from the stables and came straight toward her, a large, slow-moving but very capable man with horses and with people. She had known him all her life. He had taught her to ride, plucked her out of tall trees and deep ponds, and she trusted him implicitly. And he could probably sense her tension as easily as though she were a horse in his care.

"My lady," he rumbled. "All well?"

"Yes, of course," she replied since the others could still hear. "I need to talk to you about our departure tomorrow morning." She turned and began to pace away from the staff, forcing him to keep step with her. "I want to leave as early as possible."

"I'll have the horses ready and harnessed by first light."

"Thank you. Also…" She glanced up at him and lowered her voice. "I need a favor, Ewan. I don't trust the house servants, and I would like you to sit with the baby while we are both away from him this evening."

"Sure," Ewan said laconically.

"Come up the back servants' stairs and our door is the first one you come to. If anyone questions your presence, you say Mr. Tizsa sent for you."

"When?"

"Five o'clock. If we aren't there, wait for us."

He touched his cap, and she cast him a quick smile.

"Thanks, Ewan." She turned away from him, then before he had taken a step back toward the stable, she paused. "Ewan?"

"Mmm?"

"The evening we arrived and drove past the castle, did you see anyone there in front of the ruin?"

"I saw someone. Looked like Himself."

Ewan, who had always referred to her father the duke in this way, had taken to alluding similarly to Dragan. Griz had assured her husband it was an honor.

"That's what I thought," she said, ignoring the sudden drumming of her heart. "Did you recognize the lady, too?"

A frown tugged at his brow. "Didn't see any female. Only Himself."

Would you tell me if you did? She could hardly ask him that. Instead, she blurted. "Do you believe in ghosts, Ewan?"

He shrugged. "Don't disbelieve in them. There are more things in heaven and earth, as they say. Certainly more than the mad wee tikes who'll come guising round the houses tonight! You hold on to what you have, Miss Grizzly, and you'll be fine."

Although it was hardly respectful to most ears, the use of his old childhood nickname for her made her smile. She felt more relaxed as she walked back to the house, though she knew that would not last.

CHAPTER SIX

C LEARLY A MUCH-LOVED tradition at Cathlinn, small grinning ghouls, ghosts, witches, and demons arrived throughout the evening. Some were armed with lanterns made from turnips with scary faces carved out of them to release the light. The creatures made eerie noises before reciting some scary poem or song, complete with grimaces and shouts designed to terrify.

One group, dressed as witches with tall hats and long noses and brooms made from twigs, performed a weird, energetic dance. Another acted out a short play that finished with the demons rushing straight at the seated watchers before skidding to a halt and bowing, their muddy make-up cracking with their grins.

Griz, who had imagined somehow that the Cathlinns would merely tolerate the tradition as lairds of the manor, was impressed by the whole household's enthusiasm. They gathered in the large entrance hall where chairs had been set up for the family, and the servants watched from behind, or from the front door or the stairs. Family and staff greeted all the children with exaggerated terror and applauded their acts with genuine appreciation and laughter, before the servants gave every child a treat—oranges, apples, cakes, and sweets. And the guisers went off chattering and giggling with excitement.

Dragan murmured in her ear, "Everyone is here, all the servants, too."

Griz had noticed the same thing. In truth, watching them tonight, she could not imagine any of these people murdering anyone. But then, if human children could dress as demons, it was perfectly possible for adult demons to don the disguise of amiable human. She began to worry that upstairs, Ewan had already been drugged or poisoned—even though he had been well warned against eating or drinking anything—and that Alexander was unprotected.

Grinning, a footman opened the door for the departure of a risen corpse, a ghost in an old sheet, and a very small devil with wooden horns. A gust of icy wind rushed through the hall, and surely that was a faint rumble of distant thunder? Certainly, the sky was filthy.

"Will the children be able to see enough to get home?" Griz asked uneasily.

"They've got their turnip lanterns," Richard said.

"Pretty sure they could do it blind-folded anyway," Lord Cathlinn said cheerfully. "But there will be enough people around looking out for them."

"Hurry home, mind!" the footman called after the children, "It's starting to rain, and you'll get caught in the storm."

"That will be it, then," his lordship said, getting to his feet. "Good show, bless 'em. I'll bid you all—" He broke off as his gaze fell on Dragan, and he scowled. "I don't see why you can't just spit it out, man!"

Because he still had nothing to "spit". No one had made any move against him. Griz didn't know whether to be frustrated or relieved. But this, judging by the previous crimes, was the dangerous period, when everyone went their separate ways. The servants were going about their own business, but very slowly, presumably hoping to hear the rest of the exchange.

"I will explain all in just over an hour as we agreed," Dragan said mildly. "Once the baby is settled. Perhaps we could reconvene here? I would like your staff to be present, too."

Lord Cathlinn stamped off toward the stairs, muttering about bloody impositions, and then, loudly, "I'll have a brandy in my rooms!"

"Good plan," Richard agreed.

Griz and Dragan, clearly the pariahs of the evening, joined the general procession upstairs. Nobody went to play billiards or talk in the library. Even Miss Cathlinn seemed in a hurry to reach her own room.

"If looks could kill, I would be dead many times over," Dragan murmured. "I hope this works, or I shall have made several enemies for nothing."

Griz, who felt all the hairs on her arms rising, was desperate to get to their own rooms. She almost tore the door from Dragan's hand in her hurry to get in and bolted through to the bedchamber.

The large figure of Ewan loomed in front of her, holding Alexander in one muscly arm.

"He got a bit fractious," Ewan reported as the baby stretched out his arms to Griz, "but he liked watching the children and the sky out the window." He handed Alexander over without obvious relief. "Do you still want me here?"

"We might do," Dragan replied. "Come through to the sitting room."

Griz fed the baby into sleepiness, then changed him, cuddled him, and set him in his cot before creeping out to the sitting room. Dragan stood by the door to the passage, which he had opened a crack, and was peering out. At sight of her, he closed the door softly.

"Do you really insist on doing this part?" he asked, frowning. "Ewan could go in your place. Or I could and leave you here."

"Ewan is harder to hide. And you have to be here when your brandy is delivered." She picked up her warm coat, and Dragan helped her into it, before throwing the traveling cloak around her shoulders.

A flash lit up the room for an instant, and Griz held her breath until the thunder sounded, much closer than before. She grasped Dragan's hands. "Will you cope?"

"I will cope," he said, although she felt the tension coiling in him. "Go, or you will be seen. And Griz?"

"Yes."

"For God's sake, be careful of falling stones from the ruin. And if things are…too weird, come back. We will find another way."

She knew what he meant. "You, too." She reached up and he gave her a quick, hard kiss, before she slipped out of his hold and into the empty passage.

The servants, no doubt beginning to deliver tea and brandy and even supper to various rooms, would use the back stairs, so Griz flitted along the passage to the main staircase. Every sense was alert for movement, for opening or closing doors, but the house was almost eerily still and silent. At least the stairs and front hall remained lit.

Crossing the hall to the side door, she heard voices coming from the kitchen, subdued, uneasy. They, too, needed this matter resolved.

She slipped out the door into rain and darkness. She could not risk a lantern, so she forced herself to wait a few moments until her eyes had some chance to adjust. To protect her spectacles from the rain, she drew the hood of the cloak as far over her head as she could while still being able to see. A flash of lightning lit up the sky, and she set off at a run to the accompaniment of rumbling thunder.

It was easy enough to reach the road and to cross over, though after that, the path that led to the castle was harder to find. She had to rely on the next lightning flash and then bolted through the opening onto the path.

The ruin rose up in front of her, ancient and jagged. She slogged up the muddy slope until she reached the castle itself and went carefully forward to the place where she had found Dragan asleep on the night she had arrived. It was also where April had been found.

She moved behind the moss-covered walls, where she would not be seen from the house, but from where she could see that same spot where April had been murdered, or at least where she had come to die.

She settled down on piles of wet leaves to wait, hunched her shoulders against the hammering rain, and drew in a few deep breaths to calm herself. Then she dried off her spectacles and glanced upward, wondering how loose the stones above her were. Something screeched and flapped against her face, and she almost cried out.

Damned bats, she thought shakily as her "attacker" soared up to be illuminated in a fork of lightning. The rain came down harder, and Griz wished it all to be over.

And then she saw the silvery, ghostly lady, glowing like an elegant lamp in the storm.

IT WAS THE maid Jeanie who brought the tray as usual, though she was less talkative than before and clearly in a hurry to escape. Well, she had no idea who he would accuse. He hoped it wouldn't be her.

"There's some tea as well," she said rapidly. "Is her ladyship well?"

"Yes, she's seeing to the baby," Dragan said. "Thank you, Jeanie."

She curtsied and bolted, closing the door firmly behind her.

Ewan emerged from the bedchamber while Dragan sniffed the brandy glass and the tea, and the sandwiches that had been provided. Ewan's stomach rumbled.

"Don't even think about it," Dragan warned. He sniffed the tea again and dipped his finger in the brandy. Neither were quite right. A faint, herby smell and taste permeated both. "I don't think this will kill us, but it will probably send us to sleep. It's meant for Griz, too, to keep her out of the way."

"While someone does you in," Ewan growled. "How?"

"Arsenic probably, but there's no rule that says a murderer has to stick to the same tool. I suspect we'll find out in the next half hour." He crouched to the cupboard beneath the window and brought out the remains of the second apple pie. "Help yourself."

The rain came on harder, and lightning flashed across the sky, making him flinch even before the thunder crashed like guns and a hundred bloody images chased each other across his mind. *Memory, not reality. Stay with the reality, Tizsa, or so help me, God…*

"Good pie," Ewan rumbled.

Dragan drew in a shuddering breath and began to deal with the tray. He poured the brandy into an empty flask, shoved a few sandwiches into the cupboard, and poured two half cups of tea into the plant pot on the windowsill. As a final touch, he laid the brandy glass on its side as though he had knocked it over.

"You stay with Alexander whatever happens," he told Ewan, who ambled back toward the bedchamber with a half-eaten slice of pie.

"And you watch out for Herself or it'll be me doing the killing."

Dragan only nodded and caught his breath as more lightning and thunder blasted. He folded himself onto the sofa, thought hard about the joy that was his wife and the wonder that was their son. And waited.

The door opened slowly without even a knock.

Dragan adjusted his expression to one of wooly blankness, mouth partly open, eyes unfocused. And the murderer crept into the room.

"Where is your wife?" came the hoarse whisper, eyes darting around the room, taking in the tray as well as Griz's absence.

"As-asleep," Dragan said groggily.

"You must come with me, urgently. It's a matter of life and death."

And suddenly, he remembered clearly that this had happened before. The night Griz came when he had wakened at the castle. If her horses and carriage had not disturbed the killer, he would probably be dead already.

Dead. A thunderclap seemed to shout it at him, but at least he retained enough sense to let himself be pulled to his feet by an iron grip. He stumbled from the room, terrified he had miscalculated, that he was not up to this, not with the debilitating noise of the storm and his wife depending on him.

GRIZ STARED AT the apparition, who seemed to lean against the tall stone where she had first seen her with Dragan. Her back was to Griz, her hair shimmering down her slender back. It might have been the wind, but Griz thought she sighed.

Somewhere, she knew she should be appalled by this hallucination. Although it could also be a theatrical trick. The woman could be real.

"What are you doing here?" Griz blurted.

The ghost whipped round and surged toward her, making Griz clutch her throat in sudden fear. No human moved with such speed, with such smoothness. More than that, the beautiful, translucent face was almost the same as that in the portrait of Aileen Cathlinn.

While Griz forgot to breathe, the ghost gazed at her, head leaning to one side. *Waiting.*

The ghostly lips did not frame the words, but Griz heard them all the same, as though they had arrived in her brain without troubling her ears.

"For him? For the Jacobite, Kenneth MacDonald?"

He will come.

"After a hundred years?"

The ghostly head jerked back. *A hundred years… Is he dead?*

A wealth of tragedy echoed in Griz's mind with the words. She nodded slowly. "Yes, he is long dead." She swallowed. "So are you."

Mostly, the ghost whispered. *Only tears remain.*

"Then go to him," Griz pleaded, from some pain she could not fathom, perhaps the fear of being parted from Dragan. "Every part of you should be with him."

The ghostly head cocked again. *I should leave this place…?*

"You should."

I...

The ghost whipped around, and to her horror, Griz saw that she had been distracted. Two figures were making their way up the hill to the castle, the shorter figure all but dragging the taller.

The taller she knew at once was Dragan, stumbling and falling. Although he was acting—Griz hoped to God he was acting—she hated to see him like that. Worse, just as they reached the top of the hill, lightning forked across the sky and thunder exploded overhead.

Dragan dropped to his knees, his hands covering his head as he tried to curl into a ball. She had seen him like this before, when he had no control over his body. It acted on its own because his brain was somewhere else entirely.

Fear surged through Griz, even as she willed him out of his old nightmare and into the present one. They both had to pay attention, to identify...

His companion knelt beside him, and a double flash of lightning illuminated her gaunt face and figure.

Davidson, Claire Cathlinn's maid.

She wrenched up Dragan's head.

You lie, the ghost cried into Griz's mind with a bizarre mixture of anger and joy. *He is here, he is here again at last!* She rushed on Dragan so fast there was no time for Griz to react.

The ghost of Aileen wrapped her transparent arms about him, her shimmering hair falling over his face and neck and chest. And Dragan didn't even notice.

Then, with a moan of loss, Aileen wrenched backward, and Griz could see that Davidson had a flask and she was lifting it to Dragan's mouth.

Not Kenneth, not my Kenneth, the ghost mourned.

"No, he is *my* husband," Griz cried out, launching herself from her hiding place. For Dragan in the grip of this paralysis was incapable of defending himself, and Davidson was trying to force the contents of her flask down his throat.

Davidson leapt to her feet, glaring into the darkness until she found Griz. "Who's there? You! You nasty, spying—"

"Stand away from him," Griz warned. "You have no reason to hurt him."

"I have every reason! He'll send me away from my mistress! To prison!"

"Give me the flask," Griz said, advancing. "And you might have hope."

Davidson advanced, too, brushing past Dragan and all but walking right through the drooping, ghostly figure of Aileen.

Griz held her hand out commandingly. But Davidson appeared to acknowledge no superior but her own mistress. She grabbed Griz's arm in a bruising grip and hauled her closer, whisking the flask up to her face. Griz grasped the woman's wrist, appalled by her strength.

"I have no hope if you two live," Davidson panted. "Without you, no one will pay any attention to the death of that vile female."

"Vile?" Griz gasped. Thunder boomed again, but something moved beyond Davidson's shoulders, giving Griz hope. "How was she vile?"

"Pursuing my mistress's husband, trying to take her place. And he such a fool that he cannot appreciate my mistress—she is far, far too good for him—and flirts and carries on with the vile creature instead. I could not let him cast my mistress aside."

In fresh lightening, Dragan loomed behind Davidson, plucking her off Griz and sending the flask flying through the air, almost striking the still, ghostly figure who appeared now to be watching everything.

Davidson yelled in fury, fighting and kicking, trying to scratch and bite, but Dragan held firm, immobilizing her without apparent effort although his mouth and eyes were grim.

Until, over the woman's shoulder, his gaze found Griz.

She smiled tremulously as the thunder rumbled off into the distance. "You did it, Dragan." He had broken through the paralysis while the noise still raged.

His lips quirked. "In the words of your military hero, it was a damned close-run thing."

And then lantern light blinded her, and voices called. "Well done, you got her! We heard and saw everything." Robert and Richard Cathlinn strode toward them, grinning.

Dragan almost threw his captive at them, and she collapsed on Robert's shoulder. "Take me to her, take me to her!" she wailed.

"We're taking you to the strong room," Robert said with distaste.

Griz tumbled into Dragan's arms and felt them close about her. He was her safety, her security, her love, as she was his. She closed her eyes, clutching him convulsively.

And then a shout of outrage made her open them.

"She's got loose! Grab her!" Richard shouted.

And sure enough, Davidson was darting in front of them like a hare, not aiming for them but for the flask, which she snatched up and held to her mouth before anyone could move.

The ghost watched and smiled.

Dragan, with a yell of fury bolted to Davidson, snatching the flask from her hand and seizing her once more.

"Too late," Davidson said with triumph. "Too late for all of us!"

"Only for you," Dragan said with a pity Griz could not yet match. "But I'll still try."

She fought him, of course, and the Cathlinn brothers told him to let her die, that it was only justice, and Davidson laughed and threw herself about. And the ghost came right up to Griz, her head leaning again to one side.

You will live and he will live?

"Yes..."

And for me it has always been too late. I waited too long and got lost. He was never coming back to me. I should always have gone to him.

Griz lifted her hand, whether to touch or to wave farewell she didn't know. And before her eyes the ghost faded to nothing but rain.

CHAPTER SEVEN

As Ewan had promised, the carriage waited for them on the front terrace at first light. To Dragan's surprise, the family all came out to bid them farewell. Claire even gave them a parcel of food for the journey.

Of course, they had cleared the air last night. Dragan could not hold on to his anger that the brothers had not leapt immediately to his wife's aid when Davidson had seized her. For one thing, neither had Dragan, though the threat had dragged him off his own, personal, bloody battlefield and back to reality. For one horrible, unendurable instant, he had thought he was too late, that Davidson had already poured her poison down Grizelda's throat.

The awful emptiness of a life without Griz, of watching her murder, had propelled him to his feet and into action, but he would never forget the sight of her whole body shaking with the effort to prevent Davidson forcing the lip of the flask into her mouth.

He hadn't been able to save Davidson. No one but he seemed to care. In their air-clearing session of both family and servants, Claire had told them that her maid had been increasingly erratic in her behavior and subject to terrible headaches. But since she had only ever seen the devoted side, it had never entered her head that Davidson would harm anyone. The men had been slightly sheepish about their determination to believe in April's natural death. And Richard had apologized for his more personal hostility to Dragan.

"You made me feel guilty," Richard had said ruefully, later, in a moment of privacy. "Because you were doing what *I* should have. April should have been my bride, and you were the one seeking justice for her."

Lord Cathlinn himself handed Griz into the carriage with Alexander, and clapped Dragan on the shoulder as he followed her inside.

As they drove away, Robert had his arm around Claire's shoulders. So perhaps some good had come out of the whole mess.

Perhaps he muttered something aloud, or she just read it in his face, for Griz said, "The truth is important."

"I suspect Davidson had some brain infection. Or a tumor, perhaps. At least they will do a proper autopsy."

Griz threaded her fingers through his and squeezed. "I hated it, but I'm glad we came."

In the sling Griz wore, Alexander shifted his head, and his little eyelids began to flutter closed.

Dragan said, "I will be glad, too. Soon." He turned slowly to face her. "At the castle, you said, *No, he is* my *husband,* as though there was some doubt. For much of the time, you were distracted, looking at something I could not see."

Griz considered. "We all see different things. And science isn't everything."

"No," he agreed.

The sweet smells of the countryside after rain filtered into the carriage. The horses pulled them onward toward Kelburn and Griz's large, vital family. His wife sat close to him, laying her head on his shoulder. Every day, it seemed, his life got better and better, and today was no exception.

He smiled and kissed her hair. "I love you, you know."

"I hope you know I love you, too. So much that perhaps I would wait a hundred years for you, too."

"Only a hundred?" Dragan asked, and she laughed.

The End

Author's Note

Cathlinn House and its nearby castle ruin are mostly fictional. But I confess I based the castle on an old ruin that used to stand five or ten minutes' walk from where I was brought up. It was incredibly spooky in the dark, and bats definitely lived there. Naturally, it was rumored to be haunted, though most obviously by teenagers up to no good!

Sadly, the ruin no longer stands there. Like my castle in the story, falling masonry became a serious danger, and since there was no available money to preserve it, the remaining stones were removed and stored in a Glasgow museum.

About the Author

Mary Lancaster lives in Scotland with her husband, three mostly grown-up kids and a small, crazy dog.

Her first literary love was historical fiction, a genre which she relishes mixing up with romance and adventure in her own writing. Her most recent books are light, fun Regency romances written for Dragonblade Publishing: *The Imperial Season* series set at the Congress of Vienna; and the popular *Blackhaven Brides* series, which is set in a fashionable English spa town frequented by the great and the bad of Regency society.

Connect with Mary on-line – she loves to hear from readers:

Email Mary:
Mary@MaryLancaster.com

Website:
www.MaryLancaster.com

Newsletter sign-up:
http://eepurl.com/b4Xoif

Facebook:
facebook.com/mary.lancaster.1656

Facebook Author Page:
facebook.com/MaryLancasterNovelist

Twitter:
@MaryLancNovels

Amazon Author Page:
amazon.com/Mary-Lancaster/e/B00DJ5IACI

Bookbub:
bookbub.com/profile/mary-lancaster

Printed in Great Britain
by Amazon